P9-DEX-609

PUPPY PATROL ™

MURPHY'S MYSTERY

JENNY DALE

Illustrations by Mick Reid
Cover illustration by Michael Rowe

AN
APPLE
PAPERBACK

SCHOLASTIC INC.
New York Toronto London Auckland Sydney
Mexico City New Delhi Hong Kong Buenos Aires

SPECIAL THANKS TO ANDREA ABBOTT

If you purchased this book without a cover, you should be aware that this book is stolen property. It was reported as "unsold and destroyed" to the publisher, and neither the author nor the publisher has received any payment for this "stripped book."

No part of this publication may be reproduced, in whole or in part, or stored in a retrieval system, or transmitted in any form or by any means, electronic, mechanical, photocopying, recording, or otherwise, without the written permission of the publisher. For information regarding permission, please write to Macmillan Publishers Ltd., 20 New Wharf Rd., London N1 9RR Basingstoke and Oxford.

ISBN 0-439-54364-9

Copyright © 2002 by Working Partners Limited.
Illustrations copyright © 2002 by Mick Reid.

Puppy Patrol is a registered trademark
of Working Partners Limited

All rights reserved. Published by Scholastic Inc., 557 Broadway,
New York, NY 10012, by arrangement with Macmillan Children's Books,
a division of Macmillan Publishers Ltd.

SCHOLASTIC and associated logos are trademarks and/or registered trademarks
of Scholastic Inc.

12 11 10 9 8 7 6 5 4 3 2 1   3 4 5 6 7 8/0

Printed in the U.S.A.
First Scholastic printing, November 2003

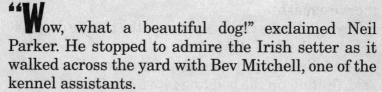

CHAPTER ONE

"**W**ow, what a beautiful dog!" exclaimed Neil Parker. He stopped to admire the Irish setter as it walked across the yard with Bev Mitchell, one of the kennel assistants.

"He's beautiful," Neil's sister Emily agreed. "I wonder who he belongs to?"

Neil and Emily had been out in the park walking Neil's Border collie, Jake. Their parents, Bob and Carole, owned King Street Kennels, just outside the small town of Compton.

To Neil's surprise, Bev took the setter into the kennel block reserved for lost or abandoned dogs instead of the boarding block where animals stayed while their owners were away or unable to look after them. "He doesn't *look* like a stray," he said. "Let's go

1

and meet him." He led the way over to the rescue center.

There were two other dogs in the center — a Basset hound that stared at everyone with sad-looking eyes, and a sort of snobby Pekingese. Bev was already settling the Irish setter into the third pen when Neil and Emily came in.

"Hello, boy," said Neil, reaching over the gate to pat his smooth red head. "Are you lost?"

The dog gave Neil a friendly look. Then he spotted Jake, who was standing behind Neil. The setter whined softly and pawed at the gate. Jake came forward and the two dogs sniffed each other through the wire mesh.

Bev unfolded a clean blanket in the plastic dog basket at the back of the pen.

"Actually, Murphy's looking for a new home," she said, fluffing up the bedding into a comfortable heap. "His owners just brought him in."

"But why? He's gorgeous!" exclaimed Emily.

"Well, Mr. and Mrs. Brown, who brought him in, are quite elderly," Bev explained. "They said he was a bit of a handful for them."

Neil felt a wave of sympathy for the dog. "That's not fair," he said indignantly. He slipped through the gate into the pen and ran his hand over Murphy's glossy coat. "They should have known before they bought him that Irish setters need lots of attention," he said.

"People don't always think ahead," Bev remarked. She patted the side of the basket and called to Murphy. "Your bed's ready now, boy. Come and see what you think of it."

Murphy ambled over and gave the basket a thorough sniff before stepping into it. Then he turned around in a circle and flopped down with a contented sigh.

"Comfortable enough for you?" asked Emily with a grin.

Murphy's tail thudded against the side of the basket. He looked at Emily with an intelligent expression and gave a short, happy bark.

"I think that means yes!" Neil laughed. He dug in his pocket for one of the dog biscuits he always carried and dropped it next to the basket.

Murphy crunched it up, then looked eagerly at Neil, hoping for another.

"He's really friendly," said Emily from outside the pen. "I don't think you're a handful at all," she added.

Bev reached over and stroked Murphy's back. "He does seem to be a pleasure to have around," she agreed. She looked at the Bassett hound and the Pekingese. "And he might be able to cheer these two up."

"Let's hope so." Neil grinned. "I've had no luck so far. They don't even want to go for walks."

Just then, Carole Parker and Mike Turner came in. Mike was the local vet. He held a dog clinic at King Street every Saturday morning.

"Hi, you two," said Carole. "Mike's here to look at Murphy." She turned to Bev. "By the way — that bulldog pup Roger in kennel block one has chewed up his blanket again."

Bev groaned. "Little rascal! At this rate, we'll have no bedding left." She went to the door. "This time I'm giving him an old sack to sleep on — and a chew toy to keep those jaws busy."

Mike joined Neil in pen number three. Murphy jumped up at once to meet him. He swished his feathery tail and licked the vet's outstretched hand.

Mike crouched down in front of him and patted his chest. "You're very affectionate, aren't you, fellow?" He grinned, then took his stethoscope out of his bag and listened to Murphy's heart. He checked his eyes

and ears, looked inside his mouth, and felt his belly.
"He's fine," said Mike, standing up. "I don't think
you'll have any trouble finding him a new home."

"Did you hear that, Murphy?" Neil said. "You'll be
going to a new home soon."

Murphy responded with a slurping lick across
Neil's face. Then he wriggled out of his grasp and began to bounce playfully around the pen.

Neil pretended to grab him. Murphy sidestepped
neatly. Then he stood panting, waiting for Neil to
make the next move.

"You're a big clown!" Neil laughed.

"And a very energetic one," said Mike, stepping out of the pen before Murphy could knock him over.

"I guess we'd better make sure he goes to a family with children," said Carole.

"I agree with you there, Carole," said Mike. He picked up his bag, ready to go. "See you next week, everyone."

No sooner had the door closed behind Mike than it burst open again and the youngest member of the Parker family, five-year-old Sarah, came rushing in. "We're back! And the puppies are here," she cried breathlessly. "Come and see."

Neil, Emily, and Carole followed Sarah outside. Bob Parker and King Street Kennels' other kennel assistant, Kate Paget, were walking across the yard. A small white dog trotted along next to Kate.

"Hi there, Willow," called Neil.

The little dog pricked up her ears. She saw Neil and came running over to him. Willow was a West Highland terrier cross who belonged to Kate and her husband, Glen. Willow greeted Neil, then quickly turned her attention back to the wicker basket that Bob was carrying.

"Willow's puppies are in the basket," Sarah puffed excitedly. "And I held it on my lap all the way from Kate's cottage and they didn't even cry."

"You looked after them very well." Kate smiled, giving Sarah's long black ponytail an affectionate tug.

A lot had happened in Kate's life recently. Seven weeks ago, on Christmas Day, she'd had a baby boy, Noel — only a few hours after Willow had given birth to her own three babies in the Parkers' utility room.

Neil thought back to that night. It would always be one of his best Christmases because he and Emily had helped at the birth of the puppies.

He remembered the three tiny little balls of white fur that he and Emily had named Angel, Tinsel, and Star. Now they had come back to King Street Kennels because they were ready to go to new homes and people would be coming there to see them.

"Are you sure you don't mind having them?" Kate asked Carole.

"It will be an absolute pleasure," Carole answered. "We know it's difficult for you at home right now with Noel to look after, as well as all the work Glen is doing to your house."

Kate smiled and shook her head. "It's total chaos! Thanks for picking us up, Bob."

Bob shrugged. "No problem." He looked down at Sarah. "Anyway, I didn't have much choice," he said with a wink.

Sarah jumped up and down excitedly. "Can we take the puppies out now?" she begged.

"Hold your horses!" Bob grinned. "Let's go into the kitchen where it's a bit warmer. Then we'll make them a bed in kennel block one."

They went into the house and Bob carefully placed the basket on the floor. Kate lifted the lid. Three pairs of dark, bright eyes stared out.

"Hello, little ones," whispered Neil. Three stubby little tails wagged in unison as Neil reached in and patted the wiry-coated puppies. "You've all grown a lot since we last saw you. And your teeth have grown, too!" he added, as the little dogs nibbled his hands.

"And look at Star," said Emily, picking up the smallest puppy. "She looks so much stronger."

Star was the last puppy to be born. At first, everyone thought she wouldn't even survive the night because she was so weak and couldn't nurse from her mom. But Neil and Emily had fed her a special milk

formula every two hours until she was strong enough to feed on her own.

Kate nodded. "She's much better, and I'm sure she's the smartest of the three. But she'll always be weaker than the others." She hesitated. "It's going to be hard finding the right home for her."

"*We* could look after her properly," said Sarah earnestly. She glanced hopefully at Bob and Carole.

Bob frowned at her. "If that's a hint that you want us to keep Star, the answer's N-O!"

"N-O. That spells 'no,'" Sarah announced.

"Brilliant, Professor Parker!" teased Neil. "Now what does S-T-A-R spell?"

Sarah had recently started learning to read and was always practicing. She thought hard for a moment, wrinkling her forehead with concentration. "That's easy!" she said at last. "Star." She put her face close to the tiny dog's whiskery face. Star squirmed excitedly in Emily's hands, then pushed her wet button nose against Sarah's. "Hey!" Sarah giggled. "She gave me an Eskimo kiss."

Neil and Kate lifted Tinsel and Angel out of the basket and put them on the floor. Seeing them on the ground, Star wriggled around until Emily put her down, too.

"I wonder if they recognize where they are?" said Emily, kneeling beside them.

"Probably not," said Bob.

"Angel doesn't seem bothered by the strange surroundings," said Neil as the puppy began tugging at the strings of an apron that was hanging over a chair.

"Watch out, Angel!" Sarah giggled again.

Too late. The apron slipped off the chair and landed on top of the puppy. Angel gave a surprised squeak and backed out quickly, bottom first.

Neil laughed. This little pup may have been named Angel, but she certainly didn't behave like one!

Suddenly, Angel spotted Sarah's feet nearby. She scampered over and began wrestling with the laces on Sarah's sneakers.

Sarah thought this was hysterical. "Pull, Angel," she said with a laugh, twisting her feet around to encourage the mischievous puppy.

On the other side of the kitchen, Star watched her sister with her head to one side, and Tinsel settled down for a snooze, his nose resting on his fluffy white paws.

The telephone rang in the office. Bob went to answer it. Star pricked up her ears and looked at Kate, then set off in the direction of the noise.

Kate quickly scooped her up. "OK, Star. We heard it, too. She always tries to beat me to the phone," she explained.

Bob came back into the kitchen. "That was a Mr. Patterson," he said. "He's looking for a dog. I told him we have two strays at the moment, so he's bringing his family to see them."

"Three strays," Carole corrected him. "An Irish setter came in while you were out picking up Kate."

"A setter? What's he like?" asked Bob.

"Beautiful," Neil said quickly. "Come and see him." Neil and Emily led their dad over to the rescue center to meet Murphy.

"He reminds me of Red," Bob said quietly. He leaned over the top of the wire mesh and rubbed Murphy's head. "Let's hope things turn out better for you, boy," he added.

"They will," Neil said positively. He felt a pang of sadness as he remembered the big-hearted Irish setter who had come to live with the Parkers after his owner died. Red had saved Neil's life by leading him out of the old exercise barn, which had caught fire. But Red was badly injured by the flames and later died from his injuries. The new exercise barn had been named Red's Barn in memory of the brave dog.

Bob patted Murphy again. Then he glanced over at the other dogs. "With any luck, at least one of you will be going to a new home later today," he said.

"And you're going for that walk we promised you, Murphy," said Neil, unhooking a leash for him.

Murphy was thrilled when Neil let him and Jake off their leashes in the exercise field behind the kennel. He kept up effortlessly with the Border collie as they raced each other around the meadow.

When the two dogs were panting heavily from their run, Neil and Emily took Murphy back to his pen. They settled him down and gave him some fresh water. As they left the rescue center, they saw Bob and Carole coming across the courtyard with a family.

"That must be the Pattersons," said Emily.

"They look like twins," Neil said, noticing that the two children — a boy and a girl, both about six years old — looked uncannily alike, with curly red hair and round faces.

The boy ran over to Neil and Emily. "I'm Jamie," he said. "We're going to get a new dog. Dad promised we could have one in our new house."

"Well, we've got a great dog for you in there," Neil said. He held open the door as they went into the rescue center.

"We'd like a lively dog," Mr. Patterson explained, peering into the first pen. The Bassett hound gazed mournfully up at him. In pen two, the Pekingese didn't even stir from her basket. It was obvious that these two weren't going to be right.

In the next pen, Murphy was waiting eagerly at the gate to meet them.

"Isn't he a beauty?" said Mrs. Patterson at once. She leaned over and patted Murphy's soft head.

Jamie pushed his fingers through the wire mesh. The setter made him shriek with laughter by sniffing at his hand.

"He's magnificent, and he seems very friendly," said Mr. Patterson. He turned to Bob. "Could we take him out of his pen to get a really good look at him? I'd like to see how he is with the children."

"Sure," said Bob. "We'll go into the barn."

Inside the barn, Murphy bounded happily around. He lapped up all the attention the Pattersons gave him and sat when Mr. Patterson told him to.

"Can we have him, Daddy? Please, please," begged Jamie. He kneeled beside Murphy and hugged him tightly. Murphy turned his head and gave him a lick.

"Well, he likes Jamie," Mr. Patterson remarked. He turned to his wife. "What do you think, Karen?"

"He's perfect!" Mrs. Patterson beamed. She looked down at her daughter Ruth, who was standing quietly at her side. "Isn't he wonderful, Ruth?"

Ruth said nothing. Hesitantly, she reached forward and touched Murphy's head. Murphy gently licked her hand. Ruth giggled, then edged closer to her mother.

Mrs. Patterson caught Neil's eye. "Ruth's a bit shy with big dogs," she explained.

"If you're worried about Murphy being too big, we do have three Westie pups looking for homes," put in Carole.

Mrs. Patterson shook her head. "We don't really want a puppy. Especially since we've just put down new carpets in the house." She put her arm around Ruth's shoulders. "I'm sure Ruth will be fine once she gets to know Murphy."

Mr. Patterson agreed. "Murphy's so laid-back, he's bound to help her feel a bit less nervous." He turned to Bob and Carole. "I think he's just the dog we're looking for."

"Great!" said Neil.

"Well, I'm not too . . ." began Bob.

"I've had an Irish setter before," Mr. Patterson said. "So there's no need to worry. I know how much exercise they need."

"That's not what bothers me," Bob replied. "You see, Murphy just arrived, and I haven't had time to assess his temperament properly. I can't tell you much about him."

Mr. Patterson crouched down in front of Murphy. "You're a friendly, well-behaved fellow, aren't you? I can't imagine you'll give us any trouble."

Murphy responded with a short, cheerful bark.

"He seems perfect to me," Mrs. Patterson agreed.

The whole family seemed determined to take Murphy home, so Bob and Carole took them back to the house to fill out the necessary papers. Neil and Emily followed behind with Murphy on a leash.

"I imagine the Browns will be relieved to hear he's with a young family," said Carole when the Pattersons were ready to leave. "They were sorry to have to part with him, but they thought he'd be happier somewhere else."

"He's going to be very happy with us," Jamie promised as he took Murphy out to the car.

Mr. Patterson opened the back door. "In you go, Murphy," he said.

Murphy jumped onto the seat and Jamie squeezed in next to him. Ruth hesitated, then slowly climbed in and sat close to the door. As the car drove away, Murphy turned and looked out the back window.

"Bye, Murphy," called Neil, waving to him.

When the car was out of sight, Neil and Emily went back to the rescue center to clear out Murphy's pen.

"What a gorgeous dog!" said Emily, picking up the blanket. "I'm kind of sad he wasn't here a little longer."

"It's sad for us, but not for him," Neil pointed out. "He's gone to a great home."

The next day, Neil and Emily were kept busy cleaning pens and taking dogs for walks. It was Sunday, and lots of boarders had come in because it was the start of the week-long winter vacation in February. At last, in the afternoon, only two more dogs needed to go out — Roger the bulldog and a German shepherd called Hannah.

Neil and Emily took them out to the park with Jake. The two bigger dogs raced along the track while Roger did his best to keep up. After a while, Emily picked up the stocky little bulldog. "I think those short legs have done enough running for one day!" she declared, laughing. "I'll carry you home."

The daylight was fading as they arrived back at the kennel. As they rounded the corner and came into the courtyard, Neil had to blink to make sure he was seeing straight. There in front of him, walking calmly into the rescue center, was Murphy!

CHAPTER TWO

"**W**hat's he doing back here?" Neil called out to Bob, who was leading Murphy.

Bob stopped. "Looking for another home," he said.

"But —" Neil began.

"It didn't work out," Bob cut in. "The Pattersons brought him back."

"Why?" Emily asked in disbelief.

"Because he attacked Ruth this morning," Bob explained grimly.

Neil and Emily were speechless. They stared at Murphy. The setter looked as friendly as ever.

Finding his voice again, Neil gasped, "I don't believe it!"

Bob shrugged his broad shoulders. "That's what I said. But the Pattersons insist that he snapped at

Ruth." He took a deep breath. "I knew I shouldn't have let him go so soon."

Emily was still looking at Murphy with astonishment. "But he's one of the friendliest dogs I've ever met," she exclaimed. She put Roger on the ground and kneeled down to give Murphy a hug. "Oh, why did you go after Ruth?" she whispered into his velvety ear.

"Maybe she teased him," Neil suggested.

"Not according to Mrs. Patterson," said Bob. "She said Ruth was just playing quietly with her doll when Murphy started growling at her, then bit her."

Neil ran a hand through his spiky brown hair. Dogs didn't attack for no reason. Then he remembered Mrs. Patterson saying that Ruth was afraid of big dogs. "He could have sensed Ruth was frightened of him," he said.

Bob shook his head. "I doubt it. Ruth's certainly shy, but not in a panicky way that could upset a dog," he said. "But, of course, she *is* hysterical now, and Mrs. Patterson doesn't want to take any chances." He looked down sadly at Murphy. "So that means you're homeless again, poor guy." He tugged gently at the leash. "Come on, boy. Back to your pen."

"Why did you do that, Murphy?" said Neil, quickly slipping him a dog treat. A biscuit was a poor substitute for a home, Neil knew. But it was better than nothing.

Neil and Emily watched Murphy go inside with Bob, then turned to take the two boarders back to kennel block one.

As they approached the boarding block, Neil was surprised by how much noise was coming from inside. The kennel was almost full, but even so, the dogs were making more of a racket than usual. "What's going on?" he shouted.

"Don't know," Emily yelled back.

Just then the cause of the uproar came charging past them.

"Sarah! Angel!" Emily cried. "What do you think you're doing?"

"We're playing," Sarah shrieked at the top of her voice as she tore past the pens with the Westie puppy racing behind her.

Inside their pens, the boarders leaped excitedly against the wire. Hannah and Roger also instantly started barking their heads off. Even Jake, who was usually very calm around the boarders, wanted to join in.

"Stop it!" Neil shouted, charging after Sarah. "You're making the dogs crazy." He caught Sarah's sleeve and dragged her to a stop.

"But Angel was bored with Tinsel and Star," Sarah protested. "She wanted to play and they wanted to sleep."

Neil had to suppress a laugh. Trust these two to team up!

Even though the game was over, all the dogs continued to bark and yap. Neil and Emily were trying to calm them down when the door to the kennel block burst open and Carole hurried in. She looked around anxiously. "What happened?"

Neil winked at Sarah. "Nothing serious," he said, turning to his mom. "Just some fooling around."

"I was playing a game with Angel," Sarah said. "She needs to play a lot, you know."

"And she also needs to rest a lot," said Carole, bending down to pick up Angel. She returned the panting puppy to her pen. "You can play with them all again after dinner, Sarah," she said. "But in the barn, where you won't cause such an uproar."

Neil and Emily settled Roger and Hannah in their pens, then went back to the rescue center to check on Murphy.

The Irish setter thumped his tail when he saw them coming in, but his eyes looked a bit sad and puzzled.

"Poor Murphy," said Emily. She went into his pen and smoothed his soft fur. "Why did you bite Ruth?" she asked quietly.

Murphy whined softly and he nuzzled her hand.

"If only you could talk!" Neil sighed. "Then you could tell us exactly what happened."

"What are your plans for today?" Bob asked Neil and Emily the next morning at breakfast.

"Dogs, dogs, and more dogs," replied Neil with a grin. He couldn't imagine a better way of spending his time. It was just as well it was winter vacation. With Kate working only one day a week until Noel was older, Bev was going to need all the help she could get. "I'm going to take Murphy out for a really long walk this morning," Neil added.

Jake looked up at him and barked sharply.

"Yes — and you, too. I'd never leave you behind. But first we have to wash the dishes."

The phone rang in the office and Carole went to answer it. She came back a few minutes later. "That was Kate," she said. "She's coming over soon because Christine Holmes wants to see the pups."

"Christine Holmes?" said Bob, pulling on his jacket to go out to the kennel. "Doesn't she run the local daycare center?"

"That's right," said Carole. "Well — she *did* run it. She's retired now and would like a dog to keep her company. Kate bumped into her yesterday and told her about the puppies."

Kate arrived half an hour later. She had brought Noel with her and seemed pretty agitated. "This is the awful part about letting your dog have puppies," she said. Noel started to whimper and she patted his back gently.

"You mean, having to let them go to new homes?" asked Carole, holding out her hands and offering to take Noel from Kate.

"Yes," said Kate. "It'll be great to know they're going to good homes, but still, it'll be almost like parting with a child." She passed Noel to Carole, but the baby began to cry even louder.

"It must be a lot worse than that," said Neil, glancing at Noel's crumpled red face.

Kate laughed. She took a pacifier out of her bag and gave it to Carole. "I guess puppies don't cry as loudly as babies do," she admitted.

"Puppies are prettier, too," said Sarah. She was standing on a chair next to Carole so that she could get a close look at Noel.

"I know," Kate agreed with a smile. "Noel doesn't

look his best when he's crying." She winked at Sarah. "I think puppies are cute, too — especially Willow's."

There was the sound of tires on gravel. They glanced out of the window and saw a green hatchback pulling up the driveway.

Kate sighed. "This is it. The first prospective owner."

While Kate went to meet Mrs. Holmes, Neil, Emily, and Sarah fetched the puppies from the kennel and took them into Red's Barn.

Angel immediately started to explore. She trotted into a corner and found a short piece of rope. Seizing it in her mouth, she looked up hopefully at Sarah. At once, Sarah dropped to her knees and took hold of one end of the rope. By the time Kate and Mrs. Holmes came in, they were engaged in a serious game of tug-of-war.

"They're adorable!" Mrs. Holmes exclaimed. She kneeled down and patted Star. The little dog sniffed her hands inquisitively for a moment, then decided she'd rather play with Jake, who was chasing after a ball that Neil had thrown.

Mrs. Holmes smiled and reached across to Tinsel, who was sitting quietly nearby. "You seem like a quiet little fellow," she said.

Tinsel stood up and wagged his tail. He trotted forward, then snuggled up against Mrs. Holmes's padded jacket, his chin resting on her knee.

Meanwhile, Sarah and Angel were still tugging at the rope. "Pull, Angel!" squealed Sarah.

Growling fiercely, the little dog dug her back paws into the ground and yanked with all her might.

Mrs. Holmes glanced at the pair and chuckled, then turned back to sleepy Tinsel. As she leaned forward to pat him again, her scarf slipped down from her neck and dangled in midair.

At that moment, Angel let go of the rope. She spun around and bounded over to Mrs. Holmes, grabbing the end of the scarf with her sharp little teeth.

"Angel!" cried Kate. "Stop that." She crouched down and was about to pry the puppy's mouth open when Mrs. Holmes said in a commanding tone, "Angel! Let go!"

To Neil's surprise, the little dog immediately opened her mouth and let go of the scarf, staring wide-eyed at Mrs. Holmes.

Mrs. Holmes folded her arms and, in a calm, firm voice, said, "Sit."

Angel blinked, then sat. And she wasn't the only one. From where he was lying on the floor, chewing his ball, Jake quickly pulled himself up to a sitting position.

Neil was very impressed. With one word, Mrs. Holmes had two dogs completely under her control. "Wow!" he exclaimed.

Mrs. Holmes looked at him, her eyes twinkling merrily. "Oh, that was nothing," she said. "I've had to deal with much worse behavior in the daycare center than having my scarf pulled." She picked up Angel. "Do you know something, little one?" she said to her. Angel gazed back and wagged her stubby little tail. "I think you and I could have a lot of fun together!"

Emily exchanged glances with Neil. They both grinned broadly. Angel had found her perfect match.

CHAPTER THREE

Neil and Emily took Tinsel and Star back to Willow in the boarding block. Neil was still a little surprised at the way things had turned out. "I really thought Mrs. Holmes would want a quiet puppy, like Tinsel," she said to Emily.

"Maybe she misses all the naughty children and wants a naughty puppy to remind her of them," Emily suggested.

They went into the kitchen. Kate was fishing around in her big bag while Mrs. Holmes was sitting at the table with Noel in her arms. The baby gazed up at her, gurgling and smiling happily.

Mrs. Holmes isn't only good with dogs, thought Neil. *She can handle babies, too.* He remembered how miserable Noel had been earlier.

Carole and Sarah were pulling on their coats.

"We won't be long," Carole said to Neil and Emily. "I'm taking Sarah into town for some new ballet shoes. Will one of you make Kate and Christine some tea?"

"I will," said Emily, going over to the kettle.

Kate pulled out a plastic folder. "Ah! Here's Angel's vaccination certificate," she said. She handed it to Mrs. Holmes.

"Thank you," said Mrs. Holmes. "I'll just write you out a check, and then I'll be on my way. Neil, would you hold Noel for a minute?"

Neil cast a desperate glance at Emily. But she was busy making the tea. Hesitantly, he took the baby. He held his breath, expecting Noel to burst out crying, but the baby continued to coo happily. Neil breathed out. Perhaps babies weren't that bad after all.

He dragged a chair out from the table with one of his feet and sat down stiffly. Jake padded over and began sniffing at the baby's head.

"No, Jake," said Neil.

But Jake was determined to say hello. He licked Noel right across the face.

"Oops," said Neil, worried that both Kate and Noel would object.

But Kate was unfazed. "Don't worry." She smiled. "Noel's had quite a few doggy kisses already. I think he enjoys them."

Kate was right. The baby was smiling and cooing more than ever. Kate reached across the table and

gave Neil a wipe to clean Noel's face. Feeling really uncomfortable, Neil dabbed at the baby's cheek. He felt much more at home with dogs.

"Er, I think I need to see to Murphy now," said Neil, desperate for an excuse to hand Noel over to someone else. He turned to Emily. "Take Noel please, Em," he said. "I want to get Murphy ready for his walk."

"OK," said Emily. "Hey! Why don't we take Noel to meet all the dogs?"

"Um, OK," Neil said doubtfully. His plan wasn't working out as he'd hoped. But at least if they went to the kennel, Emily would probably take charge of Noel. He looked at Kate.

"Good idea," she said. "After all, he needs to get used to lots of dogs, since his mother's a kennel assistant!" She took a small blanket out of her bag and gave it to Neil. "Just make sure he keeps warm. It's really chilly today."

Emily opened the back door. "Come on, Jake," she called. "Let's go."

Neil followed Emily across the courtyard, keeping an anxious eye on the baby in his arms. Ahead of him, Emily and Jake went into the rescue center.

When Neil went inside, Emily called him over to the pen with the Bassett hound. "Bring Noel to meet this old doggy first," she suggested.

Neil carried the baby over, but the dog wasn't interested in any of them. He opened his eyes for a second, then went back to sleep.

"Murphy will probably be a lot friendlier," Neil said. "He's always glad to see us."

They slipped through the gate into Murphy's pen, leaving Jake outside.

Neil went over to the setter, who had been asleep in his basket. "Look, boy," he said. "You've got a little visitor."

Murphy opened his eyes and yawned. He stood up and stretched; then, without any warning, he lifted his lip and began to growl.

"What's up?" Neil asked, surprised at Murphy's re-action. He reached out with one hand to pat Murphy. "Did we make you jump?"

The setter stepped back and growled again.

"It's only me," Neil continued, feeling very puzzled. Murphy had never reacted to him like this before.

"What's the matter?" asked Emily anxiously.

"I don't know," Neil said. He shifted Noel into the crook of one arm, then reached toward Murphy again. "Calm down, boy."

Suddenly, Murphy lunged at Neil, barking sav-agely.

"No, Murphy!" Emily shouted. She tried to grab his collar, but he slipped out of her reach.

Neil backed away, trying to keep calm, although his

legs felt like jelly. Murphy continued to snarl, his eyes mean and narrow. Neil found himself pinned in a corner at the back of the pen. And to make matters worse, Noel started to wail at the top of his lungs.

"Call Dad," Neil said to Emily urgently, lifting the screaming baby onto his shoulder, out of Murphy's reach.

Emily charged out of the pen. Neil's heart pounded against his chest. He hoped his dad was close by.

Just when Neil thought he would never escape in one piece, help arrived.

"Murphy!" Bob's commanding voice rang out as he charged into the pen. He grabbed Murphy's collar and pulled him away from Neil and the baby. "Get out, fast," he said to Neil, his strong hands gripping the collar tightly.

Neil edged past Murphy and out of the pen, quickly shutting the gate behind them. Noel continued to cry. Neil rocked and jiggled him, but the baby kept up a steady wail.

"What happened in here?" called Bob from the pen. Before Neil could answer, Emily came back in with Kate running behind her.

"Is Noel all right?" Kate cried anxiously, her face completely white. She lifted the baby out of Neil's arms.

Neil didn't know whether to feel relieved or embarrassed. "He's fine — I think I scared him," he said, swallowing hard.

"What in the world did you do?" asked Bob. He was still holding Murphy. The setter seemed a bit calmer, but he was still growling.

"Nothing," said Emily. "We just went in to say hello and he went crazy."

"He didn't bite Noel, did he?" asked Kate. She examined Noel's arms and legs as the baby's crying got quieter.

"No. I kept him out of Murphy's reach," Neil reassured her.

"Thank goodness," said Kate, letting out a deep breath. "For a minute there I thought something terrible had happened. Come on, Noel, I think we'd better head home." She paused and looked at Bob. "Didn't you say Murphy did a similar thing with the Pattersons?"

Bob sighed deeply. "That's right. I was sure he'd been provoked. But I don't think so anymore." He stroked Murphy's head thoughtfully. "We have a big problem here, don't we, boy?"

Murphy looked at Kate. He snarled threateningly, baring his sharp white teeth. And then, as Kate turned and walked out of the rescue center, he fell silent.

"That's funny," said Emily. "Look at him now."

Bob let go of Murphy's collar. Murphy looked up at him, his tail wagging as if nothing had happened.

Bob frowned. "You're a real Jekyll and Hyde, aren't you?"

"Maybe he isn't," said Neil slowly. An idea had just popped into his head. Murphy was fine now, but it was only once Kate and Noel were out of sight that he had calmed down. Kate hadn't been there originally. Could Murphy's rage have had something to do with Noel?

CHAPTER FOUR

"**B**ut *something* must have upset Murphy," said Carole when Neil and Emily told her about the incident later that morning. "Did Noel scream or accidentally poke him?"

"No," Neil said.

Carole took a pair of pink satin ballet shoes out of a box and gave them to Sarah.

"K-U-L-L-I-N-S," Sarah spelled out, running her finger along the name of the manufacturer on the box. "That says Kullins."

"That's right," said Carole.

Sarah looked very pleased with herself. She slipped on the shoes and began dancing around the kitchen.

Carole watched Sarah for a moment, then said,

"So if Noel did nothing, he couldn't have upset Murphy."

Bob had a worried look on his face. "I don't like it," he said, stepping to one side as Sarah went pirouetting past him. "That's two unprovoked attacks now. Murphy's obviously unpredictable. I'm afraid we can't let him go to another home yet."

Neil felt his heart lurch. He knew what this meant. If they didn't find out what Murphy's problem was, Bob would never let him leave King Street Kennels. And the town council had a firm ruling on stray dogs. If they were in the rescue center for more than two months, they had to be put down.

I can't let that happen to Murphy, Neil told himself. Murphy was a great dog. He was playful and friendly most of the time. If he hadn't seen Murphy's sudden hysteria himself, Neil would still think that Ruth Patterson had done something to upset him.

Emily stared silently out of the kitchen window. Tears were trickling down her cheeks. She wiped them away with the back of her hand, then said, "Murphy can't . . ." She paused and swallowed, " . . . be put down."

Bob put an arm around her shoulders. "Let's hope it never comes to that."

"Can't he come to your training classes, Dad?" Emily suggested.

Bob shrugged. "I'm not sure obedience classes will

make a lot of difference. I need to know *why* he gets
into these rages before I can do anything to help him."

"And since we know nothing about his background, that's going to be very hard to find out," Carole pointed out. "All we know for sure is that he was
too much of a handful for the Browns."

"But that's a start," Neil said. "They might know
something."

Carole looked doubtful. "They didn't mention any
strange behavior when they brought Murphy in."
She ruffled Neil's hair and smiled at him. "But I know

you want to help. Go on. Give the Browns a call and see what they know."

Neil hurried into the office and dialed the Browns' number. When Mrs. Brown answered, Neil told her they were worried about Murphy. "He keeps going into a rage for no apparent reason," he explained. "So we need to find out more about him."

There was silence for a few seconds. Then Mrs. Brown said quietly, "I think you'd better come over and see us. Come after lunch tomorrow, if you like."

So they do know something after all, Neil thought excitedly. By this time tomorrow, they'd be a bit closer to helping Murphy.

The next morning, Neil took Jake for an extra-long walk in the park. He thought it would be best to leave him at home that afternoon — he didn't want to make the Browns feel overwhelmed by another lively dog. After lunch, he and Emily biked over to the Browns' home. The couple lived in a neat bunga-low on the other side of Compton. The minute he saw the house, Neil decided that it hadn't been right for Murphy. It was very small — hardly the sort of place for a big, energetic dog.

Neil rang the bell. "I bet Murphy felt cooped up here," he whispered to Emily.

Mr. Brown opened the door. He was a tall, upright man with graying hair who looked much fitter than

Neil had expected. Actually, he had imagined Mr. Brown would be kind of frail.

Mr. Brown showed them into the living room and introduced them to his wife, who was sitting on a sofa in front of a roaring fire. An elderly Lakeland terrier lay sprawled next to her.

"Hello, Neil and Emily," said Mrs. Brown in a friendly voice. "I'd bring you some juice," she added, glancing down at the terrier, whose head was resting on her lap, "but I don't want to disturb Keswick."

"I'll get the juice," Mr. Brown offered. He went out of the room.

"Do sit down," Mrs. Brown said to Neil and Emily.

Emily went over and sat on the edge of the sofa. She stroked the terrier gently. Keswick stretched. She lifted her head and gave Emily a sleepy glance, then snuggled closer to Mrs. Brown and went back to sleep.

"She likes to cuddle." Mrs. Brown chuckled.

It was hot in the room, so Neil sat on a chair that was far away from the fire.

"She looks very happy," he said.

"You're right about that!" Mr. Brown laughed, returning with a tray of orange juice and cookies. "Landed in paradise when she came here." He looked at Mrs. Brown. "Not that she wasn't already spoiled by your mom."

Mrs. Brown nodded. "She was the apple of my mother's eye, all right. It was hard for Keswick when

Mom died." She took the glass of orange juice that Mr. Brown handed her, then continued. "That's why Keswick has come to live with us."

"She must miss her," Neil said.

"Well, I think she did at first, but she seems to have settled in by now," said Mr. Brown. "She's spoiled by my wife, and I take her for a good long walk every day, so she gets the best of both worlds."

"Did Murphy used to go along for the walks, too?" asked Emily.

Mr. Brown shook his head. He shot a quick glance at Mrs. Brown and said, "No. I don't think I could have handled the two of them together." And then, to Neil's surprise, he came straight to the point. "We really should have told you this before," he said. "You see, Murphy was more than just a handful. When we first got him from the Padsham rescue center he seemed fine. But he gave us quite a fright on a couple of occasions."

"What did he do?" asked Neil, feeling a surge of hope. Were they about to find out the truth behind Murphy's mysterious rages?

"Well, once when we were walking in the park, he went berserk for no apparent reason," said Mrs. Brown. "Barking and snapping and leaping around. Luckily, I had him on a leash, otherwise who knows what he might have done. I had a real hard time trying to hold on to him. Nearly pulled me off my feet, he did."

"And the other time?" Neil prompted.

"That was really odd," said Mr. Brown. "He was in here one evening and for no reason at all he started snarling and snapping."

"Was he going for Keswick?" Emily suggested.

"Oh, no," Mrs. Brown said. "It was before Keswick came. I'd been in here watching *Young Lives* — you know, the soap opera that's on twice a week?"

Emily smiled. "My mom watches that, too."

Mrs. Brown went on. "Well, the phone rang and I stepped out into the hall to answer it. Suddenly, I heard Murphy going nuts. I came back in and found him in a terrible rage. But then he calmed down again, all by himself."

Neil was baffled. The four attacks that he had seen or heard about were all so different. There didn't seem to be any pattern to Murphy's rages at all.

Mrs. Brown noticed his puzzled expression. "You don't think it's something we did to him?" she asked uneasily. "I mean, we're not going to make Keswick go crazy, too?"

"Oh, no," Neil said quickly, smiling. Privately, he thought Keswick was so relaxed that not even a marching band could upset her!

At home that evening, while Carole and Emily watched the next episode of *Young Lives*, Neil mulled over what the Browns had told them. All they'd learned for sure was that Murphy kept going crazy for no apparent reason. "There's *got* to be a clue in there somewhere," he told Emily during a commercial break. They talked about the four attacks again. But nothing seemed to add up. The other day he'd suspected that Murphy's anger might have had something to do with Noel, but now he didn't think so. After all, there hadn't been a baby at the Pattersons' or the Browns'.

Bob and Sarah came into the living room with plates of pizza for everyone. "You're such a bunch of couch potatoes," Bob teased, "that I thought we'd have dinner in here." He handed out the pizza.

Emily bit into hers without taking her eyes off the screen. Suddenly, she gasped. "Neil, look! There's a new baby in this series!"

CHAPTER FIVE

eil jumped. Perhaps babies were mixed up in this after all!

"Maybe that's twice that a baby's been around when Murphy's gone wild," said Emily. "I mean, he might have seen one baby on TV when he was at the Browns'."

Bob frowned. "It's probably just a coincidence," he said. "All we can say for sure is that Murphy's behavior is very unpredictable."

"And dangerous," Carole put in. "We need to know a lot more to be able to come to any firm conclusions."

"But we've found out everything we can," said Emily glumly.

"Maybe not," Neil said. "Something must have

happened to upset Murphy before the Browns got him." He turned to his mom. "The Browns said Murphy came from the rescue center in Padsham. We could call them and find out if they know anything."

"That's owned by the Bamfords, I think," said Bob. He grinned at Neil. "Go ahead, then. I know you won't eat your pizza until you've spoken to them."

Neil ran to the office and flipped through the telephone directory. He soon found the number and got through to Luke Bamford, the son of the owners of the center. He sounded about the same age as Neil, and was very friendly.

"It's great to talk to you," he said. "I check out your web site a lot. It's great."

"Thanks," said Neil. He quickly filled Luke in on why he was calling.

"That's pretty serious," said Luke. "I didn't really get to know Murphy because he wasn't here long. Mom and Dad might know more, but they're out this evening. Why don't you drop by tomorrow? You can meet all our animals as well."

"That sounds great," Neil said. "We'll come over in the morning."

The next morning, Neil and Emily caught the bus to Padsham. Jake had been invited to go along, too. He sat in the aisle, next to Neil's seat, panting happily.

As the bus rumbled out of Compton, Emily opened

the latest edition of their favorite magazine, *Dogs and Superdogs!* "Hey! This is terrible news," she exclaimed.

"What is it?" asked Neil.

"Stephen Durham's spaniel died." She pointed to a headline that read "Farewell, Flynn." Stephen Durham was a famous author who wrote novels about dogs. He also wrote a regular column for *Dogs and Superdogs!*, presenting Flynn's comical views on life as a cocker spaniel.

"Poor Stephen," Emily said sadly. "He's really going to miss Flynn. The magazine won't be the same without him."

"Stephen's life won't be the same, either," Neil said.

The bus soon reached the end of the narrow lane that led to the Bamfords' rescue center. Neil and Emily jumped off. In the distance, Neil could hear dogs barking. Then a loud braying broke out. Jake stopped dead in his tracks. The hair on his back stood up and he stared ahead, trying to spot what was making the alarming noise.

Neil laughed and patted down the ridge of fur along Jake's spine. "It's only a donkey," he said.

The Padsham rescue center catered not just to dogs, but to any animals in trouble. Neil wondered what else they might see, besides the donkey. They rounded a bend and saw a tall, lanky figure with jet-black hair walking out of the gate.

"That must be Luke," said Neil.

Luke ran down the lane to meet them. "Hey, Jake!" he said, ruffling the collie's fur. "I've read all about you on the King Street web site!"

Jake wagged his tail enthusiastically, then froze again.

"Now what?" Neil said.

The collie pricked up his ears and fixed his gaze on a point somewhere behind Luke.

Luke chuckled. "He probably smelled the sheep. There are two in a field out back." He bent down and whispered to Jake, "Wouldn't you just love to be let loose with them, boy?" Then he looked up at Neil and

Emily, his blue eyes sparkling. "But I think we'll stick to animals he won't want to herd!"

"It sounds like you've met Border collies before!" Neil laughed.

"Once or twice," Luke replied as he led them into the yard.

The Padsham center was smaller than King Street Kennels and it was almost like a miniature zoo. Neil was amazed at the variety of animals that the Bamfords had taken in. There were injured birds, an orphaned deer, a hedgehog that had been hit by a car, three abandoned cats, two lost dogs, and an unwanted goat.

In a room at the end of the kennel block, there were several long glass cases. Jake sniffed at one of them curiously. Suddenly, the occupant appeared from behind a rock. Jake's eyes opened wide. He was nose-to-nose with a huge lizard! He yelped and jumped backward as the enormous reptile glared at him, his tongue darting back and forth.

Luke burst out laughing. "Lucky it's behind glass, Jake!"

Neil stared at the lizard. It was black and yellow and must have been nearly three feet long. "What is it?" he asked Luke.

"A water leguaan — or Nile monitor," Luke told him. "A man smuggled it in from Africa. It was confiscated from him because he didn't have a permit to keep it. And he had no idea how to look after it."

"So why did he get it in the first place?" asked Emily. She couldn't stand it when people treated animals badly.

Luke shrugged. "Who knows? But you should see what else he brought in." He took them over to a much smaller glass case.

Neil couldn't see anything at first. He squinted into the case with his face against the glass. And then it was his turn to jump. "Oh, gross!" he blurted out. Inside the case was a hairy gray spider the size of a man's hand. Neil was terrified of spiders. He shuddered and turned his head away.

"It's a baboon spider." Luke grinned. "Dad really likes it. It's not poisonous, but it'll give you a nasty bite if it's mad."

"I can't imagine why anyone would want that as a pet," Neil said, grimacing.

"Me neither," Luke agreed, looking down at Jake. "Give me a good dog any day."

"Do you have one?" asked Neil.

Luke shook his head. "Not yet. Mom and Dad keep saying I can have one soon, but they never get around to taking me to choose one. And speaking of dogs," he added, "let's go and see what we can find out about Murphy."

He took them through a door into a large food preparation room. There were piles of different fruits and vegetables on a big wooden table, and sacks of seeds and dog biscuits standing against the wall.

At one end of the room, Mrs. Bamford was rinsing some fruit in a sink. Like Luke, she was tall and thin, with short, dark hair. She greeted Neil and Emily warmly and gave Jake a few dog biscuits. "So you've come to find out more about Murphy?" she asked.

"We're really worried about him," Neil began.

While Neil was outlining what they knew so far about the setter, Mr. Bamford came in. He leaned against a wall and listened. "It's like you're talking about a different dog altogether," he said when Neil had finished. "Murphy behaved beautifully while he was here." He went over to the fridge in one corner and took something out, then slipped it into a plastic box and snapped the lid on tightly.

"It's very strange," Mrs. Bamford agreed. "I thought the Browns would be perfect for Murphy. I mean, it's not as if Murphy wouldn't have had enough exercise there. Even though Mr. Brown's retired now, he's very active," she explained. "He's run marathons his whole life and still goes out for a long jog twice a day. He was glad to have a big dog that could keep pace with him."

Neil was now feeling very confused. He'd really hoped the Bamfords would have the key to Murphy's mysterious behavior. But it was clear that they were just as bewildered as everyone else.

"Why was Murphy brought here in the first place?" asked Emily.

"That's something we'd like to know, too," Mr. Bamford admitted. "He was just left by the gate."

"That's terrible!" Neil burst out.

Mrs. Bamford took some birdseed out of a cupboard. "You'd be amazed at the things we see," she said with a sigh.

Neil boiled with anger. Poor Murphy! "If only people would get help for problem dogs instead of just dumping them," he said, indignant.

"But you don't *know* that he was dumped because he was difficult, Neil," argued Emily. "Murphy might be so bad-tempered *because* he was abandoned."

"And each time he's rejected, he gets even worse," Luke suggested. "What do you think, Dad?"

Mr. Bamford ran a hand through his hair. "I don't know." He sighed. "I guess any dog that finds itself going from house to house is going to be a bit upset. But to the extent that he becomes downright vicious — I'm not sure." He looked soberly at Neil. "If I'd known all this, I'd have gone after that vehicle we heard when Murphy was dumped." He turned to go. "Time to feed the pretties now."

"Who are the pretties?" asked Emily.

"The water leguaan and the spider," answered Mr. Bamford cheerfully. "Anyone want to see them eat?"

"No thanks," Neil said quickly. He stared at the plastic box Mr. Bamford was carrying and decided he didn't want to find out what the pretties had for dinner! He turned to Luke. "You heard the car that Murphy came in?"

"We *think* so," said Luke. "Only it wasn't actually a car. It was a van."

Neil's heart skipped a beat. "You mean you actually *saw* it?"

"Not clearly," Luke admitted. "I didn't get the license plate number or anything like that. I just caught a glimpse of a white van disappearing down the lane. It looked like a service van."

"Did you notice anything else?" Emily asked hopefully. "Like a company name painted on the side?"

Luke shook his head. "No. There was just a triangular sticker on the back window. I think it said 'Baby on Board.'"

CHAPTER SIX

"**B**aby on Board!" Neil grabbed Emily's arm.

"That's three times now!" Emily gasped. "It *can't* be a coincidence."

Luke looked bewildered. "What's all this about babies?"

"We don't know exactly," Emily admitted. "But we think babies have something to do with Murphy's rages. Neil told you about Murphy going nuts when we took Noel to see him, didn't he?"

Luke nodded.

"Well, he did the same thing at the Browns' during a TV show that had a baby in it," Emily went on.

"So it looks like he doesn't like babies," said Neil. "Once we find out why, we can help him."

Mrs. Bamford looked up from the fruit she was

chopping. "It's not always easy to change a dog's behavior," she warned.

"I know," Neil agreed. "But we have to try. We *have*
to find the white van — and its owner. Otherwise
Murphy . . ." Neil's voice faded away. He couldn't
bring himself to say what he and Emily feared. He
patted Jake, who was sitting quietly next to him.
Jake looked up and beat his tail against the floor.

Mrs. Bamford handed a bowl of chopped apples to
Neil and a packet of birdseed to Emily. "Come on,"
she said. "It's lunchtime." She smiled down at Jake.
"But I think we'll leave the sheep until later!"

Once the animals had been fed, Neil and Emily
said good-bye to the Bamfords and caught the bus
home. All the way back to Compton, they kept a look-
out for white vans.

"There are dozens," Emily complained, spotting
yet another one going past them in the opposite direction. "How will we ever find the right one?"

"We just have to hope we see the baby sticker,"
said Neil. "And don't forget Luke and his mom and
dad have promised to look out for it, too."

"But what if the van isn't even from Padsham?"
said Emily as they walked up the driveway to their
house. "It wouldn't help if the whole *town* was looking for it."

"So we'll just have to look farther than Padsham,"
Neil said determinedly. He pushed open the back
door, and was surprised to see Mrs. Holmes back

again. "Oh, no," he groaned. "Don't tell me it didn't work out with Angel, either!"

But Mrs. Holmes had only come to pick up Angel's vaccination certificate, which she'd forgotten to take with her the other day.

Angel was delighted to see all her friends again. She scampered over to them and twirled around their feet, then made a beeline for Jake.

"She's like a whirlwind," said Mrs. Holmes, looking on fondly as Angel tugged the leash that was still attached to Jake's collar. "She's always on the go." She glanced at her watch. "I must get going myself. My car's due at the garage for service in half an hour."

"Why don't you leave Angel with us and pick her up later, when your car's ready?" Neil suggested.

"Actually, that's a very good idea indeed," said Mrs.

Holmes. "It means I won't have to drag Angel around town while the car's being worked on. Thanks, Neil. I'll pick her up as soon as the car is ready." She gave Angel a quick stroke and hurried out.

The sound of Mrs. Holmes's car starting up outside gave Neil an idea. "Hey! What about garages?" he said to Emily.

"Garages? What are you talking about?" asked Emily, frowning at him.

"The white van," said Neil. "It has to be serviced just like any other car. So someone at the garage in Padsham might know about it. Let's ask Mom if we can call some garages."

Emily followed him into the office. "I think this is kind of a long shot, Neil," she said doubtfully.

"It's still worth a try," Neil insisted, flipping through the telephone directory to find the section with garages.

But ten minutes later, he had to admit defeat. Not one of the garages he'd phoned had been able to help him. There were just too many white vans. "Without a registration number, it'll be like trying to find a needle in a haystack," one of the garage owners told him bluntly.

Emily sat back in the big black chair at the computer desk and stretched. "Well, that's that, then," she said.

Neil felt very disappointed. "I'm not giving up on

Murphy yet," he said fiercely. "I'll just have to think of something else."

Emily got up to leave. "Are you coming to help Dad?" she asked.

Neil sat down in the black chair. "I'll be out later," he promised. "While I'm here, I think I'll send an e-mail to Stephen Durham to say how sorry we are about Flynn."

"OK. I'll say hi to Murphy for you."

"I'm sorry, honey. We just can't risk taking Murphy with us," Carole told Emily the next morning.

The Parkers were preparing for a day trip to Padsham Castle. Bob and Carole had promised they would all have a picnic there during the school break. Dogs were allowed on the grounds of the castle, so Jake was going along, too. Emily was trying to persuade her parents to let Murphy go as well.

"But he's perfectly good," Emily protested.

"And unpredictable," Bob reminded her.

"Not if we're very careful and keep him away from other people," Emily insisted.

Bob picked up the picnic hamper. "You won't give in, will you?" he said with a grin.

Emily grinned back. "Someone has to stand up for Murphy."

"I will," said Sarah, jumping to her feet.

Neil gave her ponytail a playful tug. "Thanks,

Squirt," he said. "Now Murphy has all the support he needs!"

Carole took some potato chips out of a cupboard. "Sarah, put these in the car, please."

Sarah took the bag and studied it for a moment. "Hey! These are named after Murphy," she said. "Look! M-U-R-R-A-Y-S. Murphy's!"

"That says *Murray's*." Emily chuckled. She turned back to her mom. "*Please* can we take Murphy, Mom? He needs to go out."

Neil nodded eagerly. "And the longer we keep him away from people, the worse he might get."

Carole folded her arms. For a moment she was silent. Then she took a deep breath and said, "He *must* be on a leash the entire time we're at the castle. And if you see anyone coming toward us, walk away with him."

"We will. I promise," Emily called happily as she charged out of the kitchen to fetch Murphy from the rescue center.

Murphy behaved perfectly all day. He wasn't even frustrated at having to stay on the leash. The only one to suffer was Emily. She wanted Murphy to have as much fun as Jake was having. This meant that she had to keep up with him as the two dogs chased through the woods and ran after the Frisbee that Neil kept throwing for them.

By the time the family was packing up to go home,

Emily was exhausted. She sank into her seat in the Range Rover and closed her eyes.

"Oh well, Em," Neil said with a chuckle. "At least Murphy had a great time."

"And I'm worn out," Emily murmured. She reached up to Murphy, who was leaning over the backseat, and rubbed his neck. "You were great today," she said. "I bet everyone who saw you thought you were the most beautiful dog ever."

"He's certainly eye-catching," Bob agreed, starting up the Range Rover.

They left the castle grounds and headed toward Padsham. Neil stared out of the window, hoping to spot the white van. But every time he saw one, he was disappointed. The all-important sticker was always missing.

"D-R-I-V-E S-L-O-W-L-Y," Sarah spelled out as they entered Padsham.

"Will do." Bob smiled, glancing at Sarah in his rearview mirror.

"L-E-F-T T-U-R-N O-N-L-Y," read Sarah.

"Thanks for the advice." Bob chuckled, taking the left turn that led to the center of town.

Spurred on by her success, Sarah kept going. "No parking. Public telephone. Post office," she recited. "Sprig's resort."

"That's Sprig's *restaurant*," Emily corrected her.

"Restaurant," repeated Sarah. "Instant flowers."

"No. *Interflora*," Neil said. "Can you put a sock in it now, Sarah?" He was getting tired of the reading lesson.

Sarah gave him a withering look. "My teacher says we have to practice," she told him. "Bakery. Grocery Store," she added.

Neil rolled his eyes. It was going to be a long drive home.

"Baby on board," Sarah said.

Baby on board!

Neil jumped. He and Emily looked out into the street. "Where?" they cried out together.

"On that van," said Sarah, pointing out the window with great excitement.

Sure enough, there was a "Baby on Board" sticker in the back window of a white van that was parked outside a grocery store.

"That's it!" cried Neil. "We've found it."

But even as he spoke, the van started up and drove off down a side road.

"Turn around, Dad," Emily begged. "We have to follow that van."

"We can't. This is a one-way street," Bob reminded her.

"Can't we take another road?"

"There's no point. The van has a head start on us," Bob pointed out. "We'd be on a wild-goose chase if we tried to find it now." He glanced at the clock on the dashboard. "And don't forget, Bev's going off duty in half an hour. We need to get back to the kennel."

Neil punched the seat in frustration. That had looked like their best chance yet.

Carole tried to console Neil and Emily. "You can't be absolutely sure that it was the right van," she said.

Emily nodded glumly. "I guess not. We've seen hundreds already."

"But this is the only one we've seen with the sticker in its back window," Neil reminded her. "*And* it's in Padsham, where Murphy was abandoned. It's *got* to be the one."

Murphy was still leaning over the backseat, panting softly at the side of Neil's head. Neil looked up at him. "Don't worry, boy. We won't let you down. Em and I will come back to Padsham as soon as we can. We'll find that van."

CHAPTER SEVEN

Back at King Street Kennels, however, Neil had to work hard to convince his mom and dad that it was worth going back to Padsham.

"Like Dad said, you'd be on a wild-goose chase," said Carole. She took the picnic basket into the utility room. "And even if you *do* find the van and it turns out that the driver *did* dump Murphy, then what will you do?" she called.

"Ask him why," said Emily simply.

"Ah! But that could be the problem," said Bob. He squirted some dish-washing detergent into the kitchen sink, then helped Sarah climb onto a stool so she could wash the picnic mugs and plates. "You don't know how he'll react to you."

"He'll probably be really embarrassed," said Neil.

He began drying the mugs that Sarah was stacking on the draining board. "Rinse them off, Squirt," he complained, holding a soapy cup under the running tap.

"But what if he's more aggressive than that?" Carole asked, coming back into the kitchen. "Let's face it, someone who abandons a dog might not be a very nice person."

Neil had to admit this was true. He thought about the Doberman, Brutus, that they'd recently helped find a new home for. Brutus had been very vicious at first, but it turned out that he'd belonged to a man who had treated him very badly.

The phone rang and Emily went to answer it. She returned, smiling broadly. "We're going to Padsham again tomorrow," she announced. "Luke Bamford wants Neil and me to help him set up a web site for their rescue center."

"How very convenient," Bob said with a grin.

"Mmm. A perfect excuse," agreed Carole.

"For what?" asked Neil innocently.

"You know what I mean." Carole smiled. "But just promise me one thing."

"What's that?" asked Emily.

"That you won't get into any trouble on your great white van hunt!"

"We *must* find the van today," Neil told Luke and Emily at the Bamfords' rescue center the following morning. It was already Friday and their vacation was almost over. Once they were back at school on Monday they'd have little chance to go out looking for Murphy's original owner.

"OK," said Luke. "The web site can wait for another day. Let's go straight to that grocery store and find out what the owner knows."

"But that means Neil won't have time to cuddle the spider," Emily joked.

Neil made a face at her. "Feel free to cuddle it yourself. We'll wait for you."

On the way to the center of town, Jake kept stopping to investigate all the unfamiliar smells.

"Come on, boy," said Neil impatiently when Jake pulled him over to yet another lamppost. "Surely if you've smelled one pole, you've smelled them all."

"Depends on who passed by last!" Luke said with a smile.

Eventually they reached the main shopping street.

"The grocery store is on that corner," said Luke, pointing ahead.

Neil scanned the street in front of the shop. He had convinced himself that the van belonged to the owner and would be parked right outside. But there was no sign of it.

They went over to the shop and stood outside while they decided on their next move.

"We could ask inside if they know anyone who drives a white van and has a baby," Emily suggested.

"Why don't we just say we're looking for the owner of an Irish setter?" asked Luke.

Neil shook his head. "Not a good idea. If the owner *is* Murphy's first owner, he'll never admit to it if he suspects we're on to him."

"Good thinking," said Luke.

They went inside. Behind the counter stood a short, plump man. He looked up as they approached him. "May I help you?" he asked, casting a disapproving look at Jake.

He doesn't like dogs! thought Neil instantly. *He's the man we're looking for!*

Emily smiled at the man. "We're sorry to bother you," she said politely. "But we were wondering if you knew anyone who drives a white van and has a baby."

The grocer looked perplexed. "That's a strange request," he said. "Can't say that I do."

Neil's heart sank. Had they come to another dead end?

Just then the grocer looked up. "Oh, wait," he said. "What am I talking about? Of course I know someone like that. The plumber, Lee Frewin. He was just in here yesterday fixing a water leak." He scooped up a handful of sprouts and put them in a plastic bag. "He mentioned that he was a father now."

Neil nearly shouted out in triumph. "Thanks, sir," he said as they turned to go. "You've really helped us."

"I don't know how," said the bemused grocer. Then

he pointed to a "No Dogs" sign on the wall. "But you could help *me* by not bringing your dog in here next time."

"Sorry," Neil said. Maybe the man didn't really dislike dogs. He just didn't want them near his fruits and vegetables.

They ran to a nearby public telephone booth and crammed inside. Luke grabbed the Yellow Pages and quickly turned to the section on plumbers.

"There it is," said Neil, looking over Luke's shoul-

der. He pointed to a big ad in the center of the page. It read:

LEE FREWIN.
A PIPE OR A TAP, A FLOOD OR A SPOT —
WE FIX THE LOT.

Luke dropped some coins into the slot and dialed the number. "Who's doing the talking?" he asked.

"I will," Emily offered. She took the receiver from Luke. "Hello. Is this Mrs. Frewin?" she asked after a few moments. "My name's Emily Parker. I'm sorry to disturb you. I'm from a boarding kennel and I'm trying to trace the owners of a dog we have with us at the moment." She paused and took a deep breath, then said clearly, "An Irish setter."

Neil watched Emily's face closely as she listened to the reply. She looked at him and Luke and shook her head sadly. It seemed Mrs. Frewin didn't know anything about Murphy.

"I'm sorry," said Emily when it was her turn to speak again. "But we really thought you used to have an Irish setter." Sounding more desperate, she added, "You see, he's in danger of being put down. We just want to help him."

Neil squashed up next to Emily. He put his ear close to the receiver so that he could just hear Mrs. Frewin's reply.

"Put down?" echoed the voice at the other end of the line. "Are you sure?" The woman sounded as if she was genuinely upset by the news.

Emily swallowed. "Yes. You see, he keeps attacking people and we don't know why. We need to trace his first owners so they can tell us what's wrong with him." She crossed her fingers. "We're not going to get anyone into trouble. But we *have* to know about his past. Otherwise we can't help him."

For a moment, Mrs. Frewin was silent. Neil held his breath. He pressed his ear closer to the receiver. In the background he could hear a baby crying. And then Mrs. Frewin spoke again. "I think you'd better come over. I live at number eighteen, Rosemary Lane."

As Emily hung up the phone, Neil turned to Luke. He raised a triumphant fist into the air and said, "We're going to visit Mrs. Frewin!"

"Great!" said Luke. "Where does she live?"

Emily repeated the address.

"That's not far away," said Luke. He held the door of the phone booth open for them and they set off back the way they had come.

The Frewins' house was on a modern housing estate not far from the rescue center.

"I'm surprised they had to *drive* Murphy to the center," said Emily as they walked up the front path.

Neil knocked on the door. "They probably wanted to make a quick getaway," he said bluntly. In his mind, he had formed a picture of a hard-hearted couple who probably didn't even make a backward glance when they dumped Murphy.

But the woman who opened the door didn't look hard-hearted at all. Just exhausted. There were dark circles under her eyes and a strained look on her face. Neil judged her to be about the same age as his mom.

"I'm Neil Parker," he said politely. "And this is my sister, Emily, and our friend Luke . . ." He paused. "From the Padsham rescue center."

The woman gave Luke a fleeting look, then said, "I'm Elizabeth Frewin. Please come inside." Then she noticed Jake. "Oh, dear. I didn't realize you'd have a dog with you." She frowned. "Um, I think he'd better stay outdoors. As long as the front gate is closed, he'll be safe here."

Neil reluctantly told Jake to stay. *I wonder what Mrs. Frewin has against dogs?* he thought as he followed the others into a living room that was cluttered with all sorts of baby equipment.

"Take a seat," said Mrs. Frewin, picking up a pile of tiny clothes from the sofa.

They sat down and Emily began to explain why they had come. "We need to find . . ." But she was interrupted by the sound of a baby crying upstairs.

Mrs. Frewin jumped to her feet. "Oh, dear," she said again, sounding flustered. "That's Faye crying. I'd better go get her." She hurried out of the room and returned with the baby in her arms.

"She's so pretty," said Emily, going over and gazing at the tiny golden-haired baby.

Mrs. Frewin smiled proudly. "She's all we ever wanted." She ran a finger lightly across the baby's pink cheeks. "Aren't you, Faye?"

Neil found that hard to understand. A crying baby wasn't exactly his idea of fun!

"May I hold her?" Emily asked.

"Well, I — um — perhaps — " Mrs. Frewin stammered. She hugged her baby closer to her, then took a deep breath. "I suppose it'll be all right," she said at last. "But you'll have to sit down."

Emily sat on the sofa and Mrs. Frewin nervously put Faye in her arms. "Don't drop her," she said hastily. "And don't hold her too tightly, otherwise she can't breathe properly. And don't move too suddenly. She doesn't like it."

Neil had to look away. Mrs. Frewin was a real nervous wreck! He knew that if he caught Emily's eye, he'd burst out laughing.

Mrs. Frewin sat down next to Emily. "Keep her head supported," she instructed.

Neil risked a quick glance. Emily was hardly breathing. And she looked as stiff as a plank of wood.

Neil cleared his throat. "We came to ask you about Murphy."

"Murphy?" echoed Mrs. Frewin, not taking her eyes off Faye.

"Yes. The Irish setter," said Emily.

"You mean *Sinbad*?" said Mrs. Frewin. "That's what we called our Irish setter."

Neil was thrilled. The Frewins *had* owned a setter!

"So that's his real name," said Luke. "Mr. and Mrs. Brown called him Murphy."

A sad expression passed across Mrs. Frewin's face. "Murphy? I suppose it's not a bad name." She paused, then said very softly, "But I'll always think of him as Sinbad."

Neil was baffled. Mrs. Frewin was talking as if she missed Murphy — as if she'd really loved him. "Why did you leave him at the rescue center?" he asked carefully.

Mrs. Frewin didn't answer. She slipped her finger into Faye's tiny hand. The baby gripped it tightly.

Neil tried to think of something to say to break the silence. "He's a great dog," he said. "Really friendly and well behaved most of the time."

Mrs. Frewin nodded. "I know," she said slowly. "For two years he was absolutely marvelous — like a child to us, really. But it all began to go wrong when," — she hesitated — "when Faye came along."

"What happened?" Emily prompted gently.

Mrs. Frewin stroked Faye's head. "It's hard to say, really. I've often asked myself the same thing. You see, we adored Sinbad. So it was a big disappointment when he started reacting so badly to the baby."

"What did he do?" Luke asked curiously.

"He kept wanting to sniff Faye," said Mrs. Frewin. She dabbed the baby's mouth with a clean bib.

Neil was taken aback. "Is that all?"

"Well, Sinbad's a big dog, isn't he?" said Mrs. Frewin, defensively. "I couldn't let him come too close to Faye. She might have picked up some germs from him — or worse, he might have hurt her. I had to smack him away every time he came near."

"*Smack him away?*" Neil echoed in disbelief. "But

he was only being curious. He didn't mean her any harm."

"But he *did,*" Mrs. Frewin insisted. "He even started growling at her. And one day, he snapped when I pushed him away. After that, I was on edge all the time, in case he bit her."

"But how do you *know* he wanted to bite her?" protested Luke. He was looking just as flabbergasted as Neil. "He might have just been faking aggression to get your attention. Or he could have picked up that you were nervous, and this made him feel jittery, too."

Neil was impressed by Luke's suggestions. They made good sense.

"Well, I couldn't take the risk, could I?" Mrs. Frewin replied. She eased Faye out of Emily's arms. It seemed she'd allowed Emily to hold her for long enough. "I mean, we waited so long for Faye. I'd never let any harm come to her."

As if on cue, the baby started to wail. Mrs. Frewin looked agitated. She rocked Faye back and forth, but the baby sobbed even louder.

"Oh, dear! What is it, my precious?" murmured Mrs. Frewin. She lifted Faye on to her shoulder and patted her back. "Have you got the hiccups?"

Faye howled louder.

"What about trying a pacifier?" Emily suggested.

"The pacifier. Yes. Where is it?" said Mrs. Frewin,

looking wildly around the room. "It must be upstairs in her crib."

Neil couldn't bear the shrill crying any longer. "I'll get it," he volunteered, shooting out of the room and up the stairs.

On the landing he came to a sudden halt. It was like being in a gallery devoted to Murphy. Framed pictures of the Irish setter lined the walls and filled the windowsill. There were photographs of Murphy — or Sinbad, as he was then — as a tiny puppy, as a gangly five-month-old, and fully grown; pictures of him sleeping in his basket, running on a beach, stretched out in front of the fire, digging in the snow, splashing through a river.

Suddenly, everything fell into place for Neil. The Frewins had adored Murphy. But the baby had taken his place. And the more Murphy tried to find his way back into his owners' hearts, the more they rejected him and chased him away from the baby.

Not surprisingly, Murphy started to distrust the baby. Then his distrust turned to fear and anger. And now he went into a rage at the sight of any baby — even one crying on TV or something that looked like one. "Like Ruth's doll," Neil said aloud.

He felt outraged. If the Frewins had just stopped to think, they might have worked out what the problem was. But then, as he looked around at the photographs again, he realized that the Frewins must have loved Murphy very much. *They were probably heartbroken when they left him,* he thought.

Neil studied a close-up of the setter's beautiful face. "We can't really blame them," he said softly. "They just didn't understand you very well, Murphy. But it's all going to be OK now."

CHAPTER EIGHT

Neil wanted to be absolutely certain of the facts when he went back downstairs. "So that's why you left Murphy outside the Bamfords'?" he said to Mrs. Frewin, handing her the pacifier.

Mrs. Frewin popped the pacifier into the baby's mouth. "That's better, isn't it?" she crooned as the crying stopped. She looked at Neil. "I know it was cowardly. But we were desperate. Faye was sickly and weak when she was younger and she cried all the time. We could never sleep. The second time Sinbad snapped at her was the last straw. We just bundled him into the van and left him at the rescue center. We knew he'd be cared for there."

"It would have helped a lot if you'd told us the problem," said Luke.

"And Murphy might not be in so much trouble now," Emily pointed out.

Mrs. Frewin carefully lowered Faye into a pretty blue baby carriage. Without looking up she said, "But you see, that's what we were trying to avoid. I was worried that if people knew about Sinbad's bad temper, he'd never find a new home. And we were totally ashamed. We didn't want to admit what an awful thing we'd done." She tiptoed away from the carriage and sat down next to Emily. "Now I know we were wrong. But at the time, we just couldn't think clearly."

Neil couldn't help feeling a little sorry for her. He thought back to when he took Noel into Murphy's pen. It had been really scary when the big dog was snarling at the baby. Right then, Neil hadn't been able to think all that clearly, either.

Mrs. Frewin pushed a wisp of hair out of her eyes. "We really messed everything up, didn't we? And now, because of us, Sinbad's life is in danger. I'll never forgive myself."

"No, it's not," Neil said at once. "Not if I can help it. Murphy isn't vicious at all. He *learned* to react like that. And I'm going to help him to *unlearn* that behavior."

Back at King Street Kennels, Bob and Carole listened attentively while Neil and Emily told them what they'd learned from Mrs. Frewin.

"No wonder the poor dog flies off the handle so easily," said Bob when he'd heard the full story. "Now that we understand the problem, the next thing is to find a way to help him. Any ideas, Neil?"

"Lots," said Neil, who had thought of nothing else on the bus ride home. "But I think the best thing will be to use Jake and one of Sarah's dolls. If Murphy sees that Jake isn't bothered by the doll, he might calm down, too."

Bob agreed. "Good idea. That's known as desensitization. In other words, Murphy will learn to accept babies as a fact of life."

"We can turn the whole thing into a game," Neil went on. He filled his pockets with dog biscuits. Jake watched him eagerly. "Yes, boy. You'll get some, too, because you're going to help me," Neil assured him.

He went to Sarah's room and persuaded her to lend him a doll — but only after she'd made him promise to train her hamster, Fudge, to like babies, too.

Now Neil was all set to begin retraining Murphy. "I think only Dad and I should be with him to start with," he said when he went back to the kitchen.

Carole and Emily agreed. "The fewer distractions, the better," said Carole.

Bob went to fetch Murphy from the rescue center while Neil and Jake went to Red's Barn. Neil hid the doll behind a bale of hay and took a Frisbee out of the box of dog toys. When Murphy came in with Bob,

he started by throwing the Frisbee to the far end of the barn. "Fetch," Neil called to the two dogs.

The pair went shooting off after the plastic disk. Murphy reached it first. He whisked his tail from side to side and proudly offered the Frisbee to Neil.

"Thank you, Murphy!" Neil grinned, exchanging a biscuit for the toy. He called across to his dad, who was sitting on the straw bales on the other side of the barn. "Let's bring out the 'baby' now, OK?"

While Neil distracted Murphy with some more treats, Bob slipped the doll out from behind the straw. He put it on the ground, then called Jake over. "Down," Bob said firmly.

Jake flopped down obediently next to the doll.

Then Neil began to walk over to him. "Come on, Murphy," he said.

Murphy trotted happily alongside him. Neil slipped him another treat, then, when they were only a few feet away from the doll, he sat down on the ground. Murphy sniffed at him curiously. Then he caught sight of the doll. He froze and the hair stood up on his back.

Instantly, Neil brought out a treat. He wanted Murphy to start associating the doll with good things — like games and food.

But Murphy ignored the treat and backed away fast, barking frantically.

"It's all right, boy," Neil soothed, jumping up and going after him.

"Maybe it's too early to show it to him," called Bob. "Let's see how he reacts if Jake fetches it."

Bob picked up the doll and took it to the far end of the barn — well away from Murphy. He put it on the ground, then went back to Jake.

Murphy squirmed unhappily next to Neil. He licked his lips nervously and panted.

"It's OK," Neil whispered to him, smoothing the dog's velvety red ears.

But Murphy couldn't relax. He trembled and whined, all the while keeping a close watch on the doll.

"Jake, fetch," said Bob, pointing to the doll.

Jake scampered over and picked it up, then turned to go back to Bob.

At once, Murphy started growling fiercely. "It's all right," Neil said, rubbing Murphy's tense neck muscles.

Neil's gentle touch seemed to calm Murphy slightly. He stopped snarling. Neil took out a treat, but the setter still wasn't interested in food. He was on full alert in case the doll came any nearer.

"Let's try that again," Neil called to his dad.

Bob repeated the exercise. This time, Murphy didn't seem quite so aggressive. When Jake picked up the doll, the setter continued to tremble — but he didn't snarl.

Neil wrapped his arms around Murphy. "Good boy," he said encouragingly.

Jake retrieved the doll twice more while Murphy looked on in uneasy silence.

"Let's see if he'll go anywhere near it now," said Bob. He put the doll on the ground again and told Jake to lie next to it.

Neil took a few steps toward Jake. "Come, Murphy," he said, urging him forward.

Hesitantly, Murphy stood up. He took one tentative step. Neil was thrilled. He praised Murphy warmly. "That's it," he said softly. "Now, one more step." He coaxed him on again.

But Murphy had gone as far as he dared. He sat down and stubbornly refused to budge another inch.

"All right." Neil grinned. "I get the message. That's enough for one day."

"And when you think how he nearly shot out of his skin when he first spotted the doll, he's made good progress," said Bob, coming over to pet Murphy.

"Can I come in yet?" Emily called from the door.

"Yes, we're finished for now," Neil said.

Emily went straight to Murphy and gave him a big hug. "I was watching you," she said. "You were very brave. Soon you'll just *love* babies!"

"I don't know about *soon*," Neil admitted. "But I think we're on the right track."

"That's good," said Emily. "And there's more exciting news."

"What's that?" asked Neil as they took Murphy back to the rescue center.

"Well," Emily paused for effect. "Stephen Durham's coming to visit us next Saturday," she announced dramatically.

Neil stopped. "You mean Stephen Durham, the *writer*?" he exclaimed.

Emily grinned. "The same one! He answered your e-mail about Flynn. He said he checked out our web site and thinks it's great. Now he wants to come and see the kennel. Who knows, maybe he'll even find a replacement for Flynn."

Neil felt a rush of excitement. He was going to meet a famous author! But something else had just popped into his head. "What about Murphy?" he gasped. "He'd be perfect! There aren't any babies at Stephen Durham's home."

Neil knew that Stephen lived alone. He'd often written in his column about how important Flynn was to him because he was his sole companion.

"That would be awesome," Emily agreed enthusiastically.

Neil crouched down and cupped Murphy's head in his hands. The setter blinked his dark brown eyes at him. "We might just have found you the perfect owner," Neil whispered.

CHAPTER NINE

Neil's heart was set on Murphy going to live with Stephen. But he carried on with the desensitization program. Even if Murphy went to a home without a baby, there was always a chance that one would turn up, just like with the Browns.

With just over a week left before Stephen came, Neil worked even harder than before. Every day after school he spent as much time as he could in the barn with Murphy and Jake. And after each session, Murphy grew more tolerant of the doll.

By the time Saturday came around, Neil was really proud of Murphy's progress. "He'll even walk toward the doll now," he told Luke, who had arrived soon after breakfast. Neil had invited him over to see how Murphy was doing and also to meet Stephen, who was arriving later on.

"But he still won't go right up to it," Emily pointed out as the three of them and Jake went out to the rescue center.

"That's a lot better than attacking it," remarked Luke.

They took Murphy into the barn. Neil demonstrated how calm the dog was when he walked past him carrying the doll.

Luke was impressed. "You've done a great job, Neil," he said.

But one thing still troubled Neil. "The thing is, it's only a doll," he said. He sat down on one of the straw bales and drew his knees up to his chin. "I mean, we don't know what Murphy will do next time he sees — or hears — a real baby."

"Hey! That reminds me," said Luke, fishing in his jacket pocket and bring out a tape.

"What is it?" asked Neil.

"A recording of a baby crying. I made it for you the other day when my aunt brought her baby over."

"That's great," said Neil. He ran back to the house to grab a tape recorder. Then, slipping the tape inside, he put the machine behind the straw bales where Emily was sitting with the doll in her lap. "We'll play it very softly at first," he said. "As Murphy gets used to it, we'll turn up the volume."

Murphy's sharp ears immediately picked up the sound of the baby crying. He looked around uneasily.

Neil stroked his back. "It's OK, boy," he said soothingly.

Jake also looked around for the source of the crying. He ran behind the straw bales and came out with the Frisbee in his mouth. Then he scampered playfully over to Murphy.

Neil was about to stop Jake when he realized that a game of tag might help Murphy to relax. Murphy saw the Frisbee in Jake's mouth. He made a dash for his friend and soon the two dogs were hurtling around the barn.

"Let's make the crying louder," Neil suggested.

Gradually, Luke turned up the sound. Once or twice Murphy stopped running and pricked up his ears, but he quickly returned to the game.

And then came the breakthrough Neil had been hoping for. Murphy snatched the Frisbee from Jake and ran over to Emily, who was still sitting on the straw. He plonked the toy straight in her lap — right next to the doll.

"Thank you, Murphy," said Emily, looking surprised. She kept very still.

Neil quickly grabbed hold of Jake's collar to stop him from going over to Murphy. This was a crucial moment. The game would have to wait.

Murphy sat in front of Emily, swishing his tail

back and forth. And behind the haystack, only inches away, the taped baby's cries blared out loudly.

Murphy's bright eyes were fixed on Emily. He gave a short, excited bark.

"What should I do?" asked Emily quietly.

But it was Murphy who gave her the answer. Without a trace of fear or aggression, he sniffed at the doll in Emily's lap, then put up his paw and scratched at the Frisbee. He wanted Emily to throw it for him.

Cautiously, Emily picked up the doll and held it in the crook of her arm.

Murphy showed no interest in it. The Frisbee was all he wanted. He pawed at it again and looked at Emily with pleading eyes.

Emily tossed it to the other side of the barn. Murphy bounded away and caught it in midair. Then he trotted straight back to Emily and put it in her lap again.

Neil could hardly believe his eyes. The doll and the crying were as close as they could get to Murphy. But he didn't seem upset at all. "I think we've cracked it!" Neil laughed, letting Jake go.

"And I think Sarah will crack you if we don't rescue her doll," said Emily, keeping the doll away from Jake, who was trying to grab it.

Neil had a vision of the doll being pulled in two. The last thing they wanted was for Murphy to *destroy* a baby! He rescued the doll from Emily. "We'll give it back to Sarah later," he said as he hid it behind the straw and switched off the tape recorder.

A high-pitched bark made them all look around. Kate and Sarah were coming in. Star and Tinsel leaped and bounced at their heels. Kate had come to work that morning so that she, too, could meet Stephen Durham. "The puppies need some exercise," she explained.

Murphy trotted over to the tiny dogs, then lay flat on his belly and sniffed them gently. Soon, they were tumbling around him while he observed them calmly.

Kate raised her eyebrows. "It's hard to believe this is the same dog that attacks babies."

"That won't happen again," Neil declared confidently. He told Kate what had just happened.

"That's excellent news, Neil," said Kate. "Let's hope

Murphy's just as good if he hears a baby crying and he *isn't* playing with Jake."

"Listen," said Neil, hearing a car outside. "That's probably Stephen. Let's go and meet him."

"You and Luke go," said Emily. "I want to stay with Murphy as long as I can." She turned away quickly. Neil realized that as much as Emily wanted Murphy to go to a new home — especially if it was with Stephen — she would be very sad to say good-bye to him.

When he saw Stephen, Neil was surprised. He didn't look at all like Neil had imagined. For some reason, he'd pictured a small, stocky man with short, curly hair. But the man coming across the courtyard with Bob and Carole was the exact opposite. He was tall and thin with shoulder-length, reddish-brown hair. *He even looks a bit like Murphy,* Neil thought with delight.

Stephen seemed very impressed with all the facilities at King Street Kennels. Inside the boarding section, he spent a few minutes fussing over each of the dogs and asking lots of questions. Then Bob suggested they go over to the rescue center.

There were two new strays in there — an elderly mongrel and a miniature brown dachshund that began yapping excitedly the minute everyone came in.

"I hope they're not asking me to take them home," Stephen said with a grin. "Because I don't think we'd be at all compatible." He scratched the mongrel's head. "This old guy would refuse to come out with me after the first long walk I took him on. And as for you," he said, crouching so that he was eye-to-eye with the noisy Dachshund, "I wouldn't be able to *think*, let alone write, with you around the place!"

Neil felt even more convinced that Murphy was the right dog for Stephen. "Come and meet some others," he said to him. "They're in the barn."

Inside the barn, the dogs were having a great time. Tinsel was lying contentedly on a bale of straw next to Kate while she tickled his plump tummy. He was grunting softly with pleasure, a dreamy expression on his face.

Jake and Murphy were chasing a big sponge ball that Emily was throwing for them, and Sarah was chasing the two big dogs with Star bouncing at her heels.

"We'll catch the ball this time, Star," squealed Sarah, tearing past with her ponytail bobbing wildly.

Stephen laughed loudly at all the chaos. Carole introduced him to Kate and Emily. Stephen sat on the straw bales next to Tinsel. He reached across and patted the puppy. "Are the others too rowdy for you, little one?" he said.

"Tinsel's the strong, silent type," Kate said, smiling. "If he were human, he'd probably be a poet!"

Carole chuckled. "I don't blame him for wanting to sit this one out," she joked. "It's practically a circus

in here." She shook her head slowly as she watched Sarah pick up the ball and put it in Star's mouth.

"Fetch," said Sarah.

The sponge ball was too big for Star, but she managed to squash one side of it into her mouth. Then she peered over the top of it at Sarah and wagged her tail excitedly.

"Good girl!" cried Sarah.

"She's a really cool puppy!" Luke grinned, going over to make a fuss over the little Westie.

"She's very, very smart," Sarah said proudly. "See, I'm even teaching her to retrieve."

"That's not quite how I teach that command," Bob commented with a smile.

"But it works," Sarah insisted. "Look." She rolled the ball along the ground. "Fetch, Star," she said firmly, and the little puppy went trotting happily after it. She stopped the ball with her front paws, then picked it up awkwardly in her mouth again and returned to Sarah. "See!" said Sarah with a delighted grin. "Now I'm going to teach her to shake hands."

Just then, Murphy padded over to Sarah. He sat politely in front of her and offered her his paw.

"Someone has learned to shake hands already!" Stephen laughed, and looked at Murphy with admiration. "He's a magnificent dog. Whose is he?"

Neil's hopes soared. "No one's," he said quickly. "He was abandoned. He's desperate for a home."

Stephen look surprised. "Abandoned! A fantastic dog like him?"

"Some people just dumped him at my parents' rescue center in Padsham," Luke explained.

Neil filled Stephen in on Murphy's background. He told him how he'd been helping Murphy to get used to babies. "He's not really bothered by the doll anymore," he emphasized, to make sure Stephen wasn't put off by Murphy's rages. "Or even by the sound of a baby crying."

"What an extraordinary story," said Stephen thoughtfully. Beside him, Tinsel stirred. The puppy crawled onto his lap and nudged his arm with his nose. Stephen absentmindedly smoothed his wiry coat. "It sounds like you've done a great job with Murphy," he went on. "I'm sure that whoever gives him a home will love him to pieces."

Neil took a deep breath. "Why don't you adopt him?" he asked bravely.

"Me?" Stephen looked surprised. He watched Murphy, who was bouncing around Sarah, trying to persuade her to toss the ball again. Then he shook his head.

Neil felt his heart sink.

"Actually, I wasn't even thinking of getting another dog just yet," Stephen confessed, still looking at Murphy. "He's a super animal, and under different circumstances I might be tempted. But I don't think I'd be right for him."

"But you're perfect," Emily blurted out. "You know all about dogs, and Murphy needs to go to someone who understands him."

Stephen smiled at Emily. "Thanks for the compliment, but what Murphy really needs is a family that will play with him — just like Sarah is doing now — not a single guy like me who spends all day writing."

"Murphy wouldn't mind that," Emily persisted.

"It wouldn't be fair to him," said Stephen. "Even a couple of walks a day wouldn't be enough for him.

He'd find me as dull as dishwater in no time at all. The best dog for me is one who'd be happy to sit quietly next to me while I'm writing." He looked down at Tinsel, who had curled up in his lap and gone to sleep. "Like this little fellow."

Kate looked hopefully at him. "Actually, Tinsel's for sale," she said.

"Is he?" said Stephen, raising his eyebrows. "Well, like I said, I wasn't really thinking . . ." He paused and looked down at Tinsel. "But I wonder . . . ?"

There was silence as Stephen looked thoughtfully at the puppy. At last he spoke again. "You know, I think Tinsel might just be perfect for me." He turned to Kate, a smile spreading across his face. "Would you let me buy him?"

"Let you buy him!" Kate echoed. "I'd be delighted." She patted Tinsel's head. "Imagine! One of my pups going to live with a famous writer."

"Will he be in *Dogs and Superdogs!*?" Emily asked.

"Absolutely," said Stephen, adding softly, "he'll be a worthy successor to Flynn. And while we're on the subject of magazine articles," he continued, looking over to where Sarah was encouraging Star to lift her paw, "I'd like to take a few photographs of those two. I'm writing an article for the magazine about dogs and children getting along together. Sarah and Star would make a great photo."

Sarah looked thrilled at the prospect of being in the magazine. She posed proudly with Star and, with each click of the camera, her smile grew broader. Some of the photographs included Kate, too, since Stephen had asked her to give some advice on placing puppies in homes with young children.

When Stephen had taken enough photographs, he picked up Tinsel. "It's been a very worthwhile morning," he said, cradling the puppy in his arms. "I have a perfect new companion, I've taken lots of photos, and I've met the King Street crowd!"

"Just call us the Puppy Patrol," Emily said with a chuckle. "Everyone else does."

"A great name for those who guard our canine friends," Stephen replied, smiling. He patted Murphy, who was standing at Emily's side. "Lucky for you they were around, wasn't it, boy?" He turned to Neil. "Let me know what happens to him." Then he went back to the house with Kate, Bob, and Carole to sort out the paperwork for Tinsel.

Neil, Emily, and Luke took Murphy back to his pen in the rescue center. "Sorry we couldn't persuade Stephen to take you home," said Neil as Murphy curled up in his basket.

Murphy rested his chin on the rim of the basket and blinked up at them with his warm brown eyes.

"Maybe it's just as well," said Emily as they turned to go. "After all, we still don't know what he'll do when he sees a real baby."

Luke agreed. "It'll be best if you find that out while he's still here."

"I guess so," Neil admitted. Then he heard a welcome sound. Glen's car was coming up the driveway. The timing was perfect! Here was the opportunity to give Murphy the ultimate test.

"That's Glen coming to pick up Kate," Neil said excitedly. "And he'll have baby Noel with him."

CHAPTER TEN

They ran back to the house and reached the kitchen just as Glen and Noel came in.

"Hi, Noel," said Neil, taking hold of one of his pudgy little hands. "We've got an important job for you."

"What's that?" asked Kate suspiciously. She was just putting Stephen's check for tinsel into her bag.

Neil hesitated. He didn't think Kate would easily let Noel go anywhere near Murphy again. "To help us — um —" he paused. "Test Murphy," he finished quietly.

Kate shot Neil a worried look. "I know Murphy's made a lot of progress," she said. "But I'm not ready to risk him around Noel just yet." She went over to Glen and took Noel from him. "I still get the shivers when I think of what could have happened the other day."

"But he's a different dog now," Neil argued.

Luke backed Neil up. "Murphy even sniffed at the doll," he told Kate.

"But it's just a doll," Kate said, frowning. "He's bound to notice the difference with a real baby."

"He didn't see the difference when Ruth was playing with her doll," Emily pointed out. "And he was fine with the recording of the baby crying!"

Kate nodded, but she still looked unhappy.

Bob had been listening to the discussion as he made some tea. "And this time, we'd be prepared," he assured her. "So there wouldn't be any danger."

Neil shot his father a grateful glance.

Bob looked earnestly at Kate. "We really do need to find out if Murphy's cured. We'll take it slowly and make sure Noel is safe every step of the way. If Murphy shows even a trace of aggression, I'll take him away."

"I'm still not sure," Kate murmured. She looked at Glen. "What do you think?"

Glen wrinkled his nose at the baby. "I think Noel needs a diaper change," He said. "But seriously, Kate, with Bob nearby, I don't think there'll be a problem." He took a diaper out of the baby bag. "I'll take Noel to the bathroom."

"I'll change him," said Kate, standing up. Then she

suddenly seemed to make up her mind. "You can all go out to Murphy. Noel and I will join you shortly."

"Thanks, Kate," Neil said, relieved.

Neil fetched Murphy and let him loose in the field to play with Jake until Kate arrived. It had never been more important for Murphy to feel safe and relaxed.

Emily offered to keep Noel in the yard so that Kate could spend a few minutes with Murphy first. If he got used to Noel's scent on her, there might be less chance of him being upset when he saw the baby.

Kate arrived and fussed over both the dogs while everyone else watched. Then she left the field and came back with Emily and Noel. She stopped at the gate and looked nervously at Murphy, who was wrestling with Jake.

Glen came over to her. "Try to relax, honey," he advised. "Otherwise Murphy might pick up your fear."

Kate took a deep breath and walked slowly into the field with Noel in her arms.

"Can I go, too?" Sarah asked Carole.

"Not yet," said Carole. "Let's see what happens." She called Jake over to her and held on to his collar.

Neil had armed himself with the Frisbee. The more normal everything was, the better the chances were that Murphy would behave well. He flung the Frisbee into the air. It went spinning past Murphy.

The setter reacted like lightning. He leaped after it and plucked it out of the air. Before he brought it back, Bob and Neil walked over and stood on either side of Kate.

"Great catch," Neil called as Murphy trotted toward him.

"This is it," whispered Kate.

"Remember, stay calm," said Bob.

As Murphy drew near, Noel began to burble to himself. Kate stiffened. Noel started to cry. Murphy was now only a few feet away. He stopped and listened. He stared at the noisy bundle in Kate's arms, his ears pricked and his body was absolutely still.

Neil's heart was pounding. Carole, Luke, Emily, and Sarah watched tensely from the side of the field.

"Sshh, Noel," Kate murmured nervously.

But Noel wailed louder.

Murphy blinked. Then he sprang forward and sat down in front of Neil with the Frisbee in his mouth.

Kate drew in her breath sharply. Bob stepped forward, ready to grab Murphy if he made a move toward the baby.

But Murphy was only interested in making Neil throw the Frisbee for him again. He pushed the toy into Neil's hands.

Noel was still howling, but Murphy didn't even glance at him. Instead, he kept his eyes fixed firmly on the Frisbee.

"Maybe you should throw it for him," Neil suggested, giving the toy to Kate.

Kate shifted Noel carefully into one arm and hurled the Frisbee across the field. Murphy raced off after it. He grabbed it in his mouth, charged back to Kate, and sat down in front of her, his tail wagging hopefully. As far as he was concerned, Noel could have been invisible.

Neil was jubilant. "Yes!" he cried, punching the air.

Emily came running across the field. She flung her arms around Murphy. "You did it!" she declared. "You passed your test."

"That was amazing," said Luke, joining them. "I thought I knew a lot about training dogs. But you really know your stuff!"

Neil grinned and looked at his dad. "I've had a good

teacher," he said. But even Neil was secretly surprised by how well Murphy had done. Now they could get on with finding the beautiful dog a new home. "What about asking the Pattersons again?" he suggested as they all went back to the yard. "After all, they seemed ideal at first."

"They'll need some convincing after what happened to Ruth," Carole warned him.

"But if they see Murphy with Noel, that should persuade them," argued Neil.

"It's worth a try," said Bob. "I'll call them up and tell them the whole story."

The Pattersons came over the next afternoon. Kate and Noel had come along, too, to demonstrate Murphy's new behavior. Ruth was even shyer than before and clung to her mother's hand. She seemed nervous about meeting Murphy again.

"Why don't you take Ruth to meet Star?" Carole said to Sarah as they walked across the yard to the rescue center.

"Ooh, yes!" Sarah beamed. "You'll *love* Star, Ruth. She's the *best* puppy in the whole world." She took Ruth's hand and the two little girls ran off to the kennel block.

Neil fetched Murphy and led him into the field. Kate followed them with Noel in her arms, while Mr. and Mrs. Patterson and Jamie watched from the gate.

As soon as he saw Kate, Murphy went bounding

over to her. Kate bent down to pat him. Murphy sniffed inquisitively at Noel. The baby gurgled with pleasure as Murphy breathed puffs of warm air on his face. Then he jabbed out with his tiny fist, catching Murphy on the side of his face. Neil's heart skipped a beat. But Murphy just blinked. Then, to Neil's delight, he licked the baby's pudgy little hand.

"That's incredible," said Mr. Patterson as Murphy spun around and ran off to join Jake, who was digging a hole under the hedge. "He's like a different dog." He looked at his wife. "How about giving him another chance?"

Jamie had run across the field and was crouching down next to Murphy, watching him dig. "Please can we take him home again?" he called to his parents.

Mrs. Patterson looked serious.

Please say yes, thought Neil, crossing his fingers.

"I can see he's changed," she said at last. "But Murphy's not the problem anymore. It's Ruth. She had such a fright. I wonder how she'll react to him now. If she starts screaming, she might just set him off again."

"She won't scream," Jamie said quickly. "I won't let her."

Neil grinned at the little boy, but at the same time he realized that Mrs. Patterson had a point.

"Mommy! Look!"

Everyone turned to see Ruth and Sarah charging across the grass.

"Look!" Ruth shouted again. She pointed to Sarah, who was carrying Star. "This puppy is smarterer than anyone." Breathlessly, she told her parents about all Star's tricks. "She can shake hands and fetch a ball." She took Star from Sarah and hugged her warmly. "I love dogs," Ruth declared, rubbing her cheek against Star's wiry coat.

At that moment, Murphy came ambling over to see what was going on. Ruth froze, her eyes wide with alarm.

Emily quickly lifted Star out of Ruth's arms and handed the puppy back to Sarah. Then she took hold of one of Ruth's hands. "Don't worry," she said calmly.

Neil slipped his hand under Murphy's collar. "Sit, boy," he said firmly.

Murphy sat.

"Down," said Neil.

Murphy flopped onto the ground.

"Roll over," Neil commanded, nudging Murphy's side.

The setter understood. He turned onto his back, then lay still with a look of bliss on his face while Neil tickled his tummy.

Ruth was intrigued. "He's a very smart doggy, too," she said shyly. Then she noticed that Murphy was looking up at her. "He's watching me upside down!" She giggled.

"Would you like him to shake your hand?" Emily suggested.

Ruth nodded. Neil told Murphy to sit again.

"Shake, Murphy," said Emily. She held out her hand, which was still wrapped around Ruth's.

Murphy lifted up a big shaggy paw and rested it on Emily's hand.

Ruth's face broke into a broad grin. "He's a nice doggy," she murmured.

Neil noticed Mr. and Mrs. Patterson exchanging nods. He felt all the tension draining out of him. It was going to be all right.

It wasn't long before Murphy was once more sitting in the backseat of the Pattersons' car.

"I'll really miss him," Emily said as they waved good-bye. "But at least we know that he's going to be happy."

"Thanks to you," said Kate. "You know, Neil, the work you did with him could really help other people. Why don't you put the details on the web site?"

"I think I will," Neil said. As soon as the Pattersons' car was out of sight, he went straight to the office with Jake at his heels, and spent the rest of the afternoon working on the article. "Let's just hope people read it," he said to himself when he finally shut down the computer.

A week later, there was a special party at King Street Kennels to celebrate Murphy's recovery. Kate, Glen, Noel, and Luke were all invited, too.

Emily and Sarah had made Noel a mobile with lots and lots of dogs, cut out from magazines and stuck onto pieces of cardboard. Emily tied it above the baby's stroller. "Since you can't have any cake yet, this will have to be your treat," she said. "After all, you were very, very important."

Jake was also a guest of honor. "It wouldn't have worked without you," Neil told the collie, who was crunching his way through a bowl of tasty biscuits.

The phone rang in the office.

"I'll get it," Neil said.

It was Stephen Durham. "I was just looking at

your web site," he said. "I really liked your item about getting Murphy used to babies."

Neil was flattered. "Hopefully, people with similar problems will get to read it," he said.

"I can help you there," said Stephen. "You see, your information fits in very well with that article on children and dogs I'm writing, and it would be great to have something from a youngster's point of view. Would you mind if I used what you've done in the magazine? I'll put your name on it, of course."

Neil was so thrilled he could hardly speak. "That would be great," he said at last. He hung up the phone and went to tell everyone the good news. "That means we'll *all* be in the magazine now," he said.

"Speaking of everyone, where has Sarah disappeared to?" asked Carole, noticing an empty seat at the table.

"I'm here," came Sarah's voice from outside. The door burst open and Sarah came in carrying Star. "She has to come to the party, too," she said. "Because she's feeling very lonely without Tinsel and Angel."

"It's very kind of you to think about her," Kate said, smiling.

Sarah put Star on the floor and the little dog immediately charged over to Jake.

"Star's amazing," said Luke, watching her tug at Jake's collar. "You'd think she'd be nervous with a bigger dog."

"She's a plucky little thing," said Kate. "But she'll probably never be as strong as she thinks she is." She turned to Glen. "I've been thinking, sweetheart. Since she's on her own now, shouldn't we take her home with us?"

Glen was about to help himself to another piece of chocolate cake. He stopped with his hand hovering over the cake and frowned at Kate. "And then what?"

"We'll keep her until we find her the right home," Kate replied.

"Which means you'll never let her go," Glen said gently.

Kate was silent. She watched as Luke bent down and picked up the little puppy, who began nibbling his fingers playfully.

Luke laughed. "You can do that as long as you don't draw blood," he said to Star.

"Face it, Kate," Glen went on. "It's not practical for us to have another dog. We have our hands full as it is with Noel and Willow."

"But one more dog shouldn't make much of a difference," Kate argued.

Glen raised his eyebrows. "That's not what you said just before Christmas when I wanted to give poor Brutus a home," he reminded her.

Glen had been very tempted to take in an abused Doberman, but Kate had persuaded him not to.

"I know." Kate sighed. "But so far, no one has been right for Star."

Luke had been listening to their conversation. He cleared his throat when Kate finished speaking. "I wonder," he began hesitantly, "if you would let me have Star?"

Kate looked surprised. "Really? Even though she'll never be very strong and might need special care?"

Luke nodded. "I'd look after her really well," he promised. "And I know where to come if I have any problems!" He held Star up and put his face very close to hers. "What do you think, little one?" he whispered. "Would you like to come and live with me? I'd teach you all sorts of new things."

"She already knows how to sit, fetch, and shake hands," Sarah piped up.

"That means she's ready for dog university," Glen teased. He put his arm around Kate's shoulders. "I think we've just had our best offer yet for Star, honey. Particularly since Luke and his parents know so much about animals."

Kate still seemed doubtful. "Your parents might not be happy to have another mouth to feed," she said to Luke.

"Oh, they will," Luke reassured her. He put Star back on his lap and let her lick his hand. "They promised me weeks ago that I could have a dog."

Kate sat quietly, thinking things over.

"She'll never be lonely with the Bamfords," Neil put in. "There'll always be lots of dogs for her to play with. And if she ever gets sick, she'll be with people who know exactly what to do."

Neil's reasoning seemed to help Kate make up her mind. She turned to Luke. "It's a deal," she said.

Luke beamed. "Thank you," he said. "I'll go and call my parents now."

"You'll keep in touch, won't you?" Kate asked him.

Luke nodded. "And I'll even have a special section about her on our new web site!"

The following week, there was a new pupil at Bob's training class. Murphy! The Pattersons had promised to bring him back for obedience classes.

Neil and Emily went to watch the class. They couldn't wait to see how Murphy was doing.

As soon as he saw Murphy, Neil knew that all was well. The big dog walked calmly across the yard led by Ruth, who looked just as relaxed. She walked confidently beside Murphy with one hand resting on his back. Once in the barn, she handed the leash to Jamie and went to sit on the straw bales with her mom and dad.

Bob started the class by asking all the handlers to make their dogs sit.

"Sit, Murphy," Jamie ordered.

Murphy sat immediately.

"Tonight we're going to work on the sit-stay command," said Bob. He demonstrated with a German shepherd. "Now, you all try it."

Jamie stood in front of Murphy and held up his hand. "Stay, Murphy," he said firmly, taking a few steps backward.

Murphy sat very still for a few moments, looking around him. Suddenly, he broke away and dashed over to Ruth at the side of the barn.

"Murphy, no!" Jamie shouted. "Come back."

But Murphy ignored him and dived behind the straw bales.

"What's the matter, Murphy?" asked Ruth, jumping up and going after him.

Neil watched, feeling very puzzled. Murphy was being as mysterious as ever.

But in a moment Ruth and Murphy reappeared. Ruth was grinning broadly. "Look what Murphy found," she said with a giggle.

Neil looked closer. Murphy was holding something in his mouth. Neil wondered if it was the Frisbee that Murphy was so fond of. But it was a doll — Sarah's doll. In all the excitement of Murphy's recovery, Neil had forgotten to give it back to his sister. Luckily for him, Sarah had forgotten all about it, too!

Murphy spotted Neil. He padded over and sat in front of him, his brown eyes filled with trust and happiness. He pushed the doll very gently into Neil's hands.

"Thanks, Murphy!" Neil chuckled, taking the slightly damp doll and patting Murphy's head. "It looks like Emily was right. I never would have believed it, but I think you've actually learned to *love* babies!"